MURDER
BY
PENCIL

GRAHAM PARRINGTON

authorHOUSE®

AuthorHouse™ UK
1663 Liberty Drive
Bloomington, IN 47403 USA
www.authorhouse.co.uk
Phone: 0800.197.4150

Published by AuthorHouse 06/09/2017

ISBN: 978-1-5246-8237-8 (sc)
ISBN: 978-1-5246-8236-1 (e)

CHAPTER 1

THE BEGINNING

In a bar somewhere in Las Vegas, Mo Green sat all alone drinking his whisky. He had just lost five million dollars in a business deal with that low-life sleazeball Vinney Costello. Mo was born in Las Vegas in 1950 and grew up there. He was brought up on the glitz and glamour of Vegas, and he loved it. He was a proud man who had made his money from property deals while living in LA. Now divorced, he had two grown-up daughters he never really saw. He was a short, fat man who dressed really well, and he always loved wearing suits.

Mo moved back to Las Vegas after working in Los Angeles for a few years. He now lived alone on a ranch a few miles out of Vegas where he raised a few horses, but that was more of a hobby than a business. He now had a problem—a big problem: He had lost so much money.

He needed to get it back—or at least get even. He was determined to get revenge on that sleazeball who had ripped him off. He sat there drinking and plotting his revenge. He ordered another whiskey, and that was when the idea first came to him.

His first encounter with that sleazeball Vinney Costello was through a business deal many years earlier, which actually went very well, but he should have known better. Vinney Costello was getting a bad reputation in Las Vegas as an unreliable businessman. The pair was to open some new bars and diners just off the Las Vegas strip. They had found some rundown buildings and decided to put some money into them. The deal could have made them millions, but then it collapsed, and Mo Green lost all his money. He was convinced that Vinney Costello had robbed him.

Vinney Costello was born in 1945 in Los Angeles. He was a tough man who came from a working-class background. He was the only son of an Italian ship worker. His mother was a Jewish immigrant. He moved to Las Vegas in the 1970s for business reasons, or so he told everyone. He made his money in LA with some shady business deals. When he came to Vegas, he became the owner of several bars and clubs. He was a ruthless man who made more enemies than friends.

He became a money-mad guy who would do anything for a quick buck. He liked to play the big guy and hung around the sleazy sex bars and clubs of Las Vegas. He liked to mix with the low life, the drug dealers, the gangsters, and the hookers, and he was often violent toward them. The hookers hated him and would leave the room whenever he would walk in. Vinney Costello was not a nice man, and Mo Green regretted ever knowing him.

Mo Green ordered another drink, a double whisky. He now knew how he was going to get even and how he was going to sort this guy out for good. He remembered when he was over in England on a business trip and was introduced to a man who could help sort out other people's problems. The man told him if he ever needed a problem or a person sorted out that he was the man.

His name was Michael, but all his friends called him Micky. All Mo Green had to do was text a code to the number that Micky had given him, and then as soon as possible, he would get back to him and his problem would get sorted. Mo Green had to contact him through a third party.

Mo Green sat drinking his whisky at the bar, thinking, *If I could pay Micky to come over to Las Vegas and kill that sleazeball Costello, it would make me feel a whole lot better and maybe give me some sort of satisfaction at least.*

Chapter 2

THE HIT MAN

Michael Morrison was born in London in 1975. His parents were English. His family moved to Manchester when he was five. Micky had a tough childhood and never really saw much of his farther, who was always in and out of prison, mainly for violence and robbery. He was a tough man whom people feared. His mother and father divorced when Micky was about ten. His mother drifted between relationships, often being beaten by the men in her life. Micky saw a lot of this, and it had a bad effect on him. Micky grew up fighting in the streets and was soon expelled from school for fighting. Then, when he was a teenager, he quickly progressed to football violence. It was organized violence, to which Micky took a liking. He was arrested on many occasions and did a short time in prison. He soon got into drugs. He started drug running for a couple of years. That was where Micky got his taste for drugs; cocaine was Micky's favorite drug. He became a drug runner and debt collector. Cocaine and violence were Micky's menu for life.

Micky was tall, dark, and handsome—not a pretty boy, but handsome. He had dark-black hair, high cheekbones, and brown eyes. He kept himself fit. He was a dark, mysterious man and a man of few words, but he had a wicked sense of humor. He also had a temper. The women loved him. He was not a man to cross. Micky soon became the hit man for the big drug gangs. He never liked to carry a gun. He always got his weapon the day before the hit and then passed it on soon after the kill. He also knew how to use his fists. He was a good boxer in his youth, but drugs, sex, and violence were Micky's life. His girlfriend was named Carla. They would take cocaine when they were having one of their sex sessions. They both loved it: the drugs and the sex. Micky always traveled with Carla whenever he was doing a hit. He thought a couple together was less suspicious.

"It looks like we are on a holiday break," Micky would say. "They would always look for a single man, not a couple."

CHAPTER 3

THE GIRLFRIEND

Carla O'Connor was born in Manchester in the 1980s. Her parents were Irish, and she came from a middle-class family. Carla was brought up well in Manchester. She had a crazy side to her and was expelled from school for sniffing glue. At sixteen, she started hanging out in the pubs and clubs of Manchester. She loved her music, and she loved the drugs. It was at that time she met Micky.

She found him very sexy and exciting. He was different from the other boys she had known. He was not only handsome; he was a hard man as well, which she loved. They soon became a couple, and she quickly became involved in his violent pastimes, including going to boxing matches. They both had something in common: sex and drugs. Carla had the same passion for cocaine. She also loved to travel and went with Micky everywhere. She found it dangerous and exciting. She loved the lifestyle, the traveling, the drugs, and, of course, the sex. She also loved the money side of it. She loved the lifestyle more than she loved Micky. All her friends had boring lives. Carla's was so exciting. This was

Carla's menu for life. She was a stunning girl with a figure to die for and had beautiful, long, dark hair. All the men loved her, but she was Micky's girlfriend, and everyone knew it. Wherever Micky went, Carla went. As Micky said, "No one notices a couple."

CHAPTER 4

THE CONTACT

Mo Green had made his mind up: He was going to have Vinney Costello killed, and he wanted it done has soon as possible. He wanted the Englishman called Micky the Hit Man to do it. He had the contact number and the secret code. All he had to do was text the number and put the code in. Mo Green ordered another whisky and drank it quickly. His hands were shaking, and he was sweating. His heart was racing. He ordered another whisky, knocking it back in one.

He was now ready to make contact with Micky. He got up and left the bar. He then made his way outside where he waved a taxi over. He got in the taxi and ordered the driver to take him to his office. It was only a ten-minute drive. Once he was in his office, he went to the safe where he kept a mobile phone for business and private use only. No one knew about the phone. He then found the number the Englishman called Micky had given him. He was now ready to make contact.

Mo got the number up and then the code: "PENCIL." That was all he had to do—text and send. He didn't know why the code was PENCIL, but that was all he was told to text. Then he would wait.

He sent the text. It could be hours, it could be days, or it could be weeks before he got a response. Mo sat back in his chair. He had done it.

He got up and poured himself a large whisky and then sat back down in his chair. Contact was made.

Hours later, Mo was woken by the mobile phone ringing. He had fallen asleep. He looked at his watch. He had been asleep for six hours. He picked up the phone and answered. It was Micky.

They talked for a short time and then agreed to a fee and which hotel he would stop at. He was to be booked in as a couple on holiday in Vegas, so as not to raise suspicion. For Micky and Carla, it would be natural. They would stop at Caesars Palace. The flights and hotel would be booked by Carla so it could not be linked to Mo Green. All he had to pay for was for the hit. All the dates for the flights and the hotel were agreed upon. It took a thirty-minute phone call, and the hit was on, Vinney Costello's fate had been sorted. It would cost Mo Green $75,000. The date was set. In one week, Micky would be in Las Vegas.

CHAPTER 5

THE ARRIVAL

Waiting at the Las Vegas airport, Mo Green was nervous and sweating as he waited for the Englishman Micky to arrive on the flight from Manchester. As he paced up and down, the passengers started to come through the arrival area. His wait was over.

Micky walked through the arrivals section followed by Carla. They both walked calmly through, carrying their luggage. Micky looked really cool, at six foot one with his handsome looks and suntanned skin. He was dressed in a white linen shirt and pants and wore designer sunglasses. He looked more like a Hollywood film star that a killer. Carla was walking alongside him, looking sexy in her tight-fitting, low-cut white jumpsuit. She looked stunning. Both of them looked like films stars.

Mo went over to greet them. He shook hands with Micky and hugged and kissed Carla. Mo led them outside and over to the parking garage. They all got in the car, and Mo drove them over to Caesars Palace. They soon arrived at the hotel.

Mo parked outside the main door, and the doorman came over to help them with their luggage. Carla stepped out to tell the doorman what to take in, while Micky' talked to Mo Green in the car.

"This is how it's going to be," Micky said. "We will holiday here for five days, just like a normal couple. We will gamble in the casinos, we will drink at the bar, we will sunbathe around the pool, we will take in a couple of shows, and we will mix with people—just like a normal ordinary couple on holiday.

"Then, after five days, I will contact you about the job, and we will talk about it. Don't contact me. I will contact you. Do you understand, Mo? Have you got that?"

"Yes," Mo said. "I understand."

"Good. I will see you in five days," Micky said. "Timing is everything in this job. Micky is never late for any meeting or job. You got that, Mo?" Micky got out of the car, and Mo Green drove off.

Micky and Carla headed in to the hotel to check in at the reception desk. When they were done, they headed up to the room. Carla unlocked the door, and they were soon unpacking.

"Can we have one of our sessions while we are in Vegas, Micky?" Carla asked.

"Of course we can, Carla," said Micky. "I can't see why not. I'll see what I can do. I'll sort the gear out, you look for the hunk, and we will have some sexy fun."

Wherever Micky and Carla went on vacation or for work, they had what they call a session, which always included a third party and was a drug-filled orgy in their room. Micky sorted the drugs out, Carla picked the man or woman. It didn't matter to Carla. It was just a threesome—just sex and cocaine.

Micky and Carla loved sex, and the combination of sex, drugs, and killing was the buzz they both needed. Micky had a big sex drive and a cock to match it. Carla also had a large sex drive—even more than Micky. Men or women, it wasn't a problem. She would burn Micky out all the time, Micky would always take part, but when he was done, he would sit back and watch the show. He loved watching Carla fuck someone else. It turned them both on. Carla also liked to watch Micky fucking someone else. That was there sex menu. Lust for life, Micky would say. They were both a good match in the bedroom. Carla would go at it all night, and Micky loved it. On trips, they were always searching for a good-looking man or woman, or a couple, for their session. The sex, the drugs, and the killing—it was a dangerous life, but that was what Micky and Carla loved. It was their menu for life.

CHAPTER 6

THE HOLIDAY

Three days later the holiday was going well, and Micky and Carla had mixed in well with most of the hotel guests. They had sunbathed around the pool, been drinking at the many hotel bars, and gone gambling in the hotel casinos. They even took in a couple of shows on the Vegas Strip. Micky loved his music, and so did Carla. They visited the famous gangster museum and the film stars museum and took a trip down to the old Las Vegas where Carla went and did some clothes shopping and bought Micky some shirts. They also went bar hopping down on the Strip. They visited the Grand Canyon and took a helicopter flight around Vegas. As planned, they blended in just like any other normal English couple. No one suspected anything. They were just Micky and Carla from Manchester having a great time in Las Vegas.

Micky had made friends with one of the hotel staff named Brad. He worked behind the bar and around the pool area, and he soon caught Carla's eye. She would sit at the pool bar and flirt with him. At night, he worked in the lounge bar, and when he finished his shift, he would always sit and drink with them. Brad was a good-looking guy— tall, muscular, and dark-skinned. He was half Mexican but had been born in Vegas. He was always smiling, and Carla had the hots for him. Carla was thinking about her sex session, her threesome, and decided she wanted Brad. She told Micky too sort it out, which he did.

CHAPTER 7

THE SEX PARTY

The following night Carla was all ready for her sex party. This was their fourth day in Vegas. She had showered and done her hair. She was wearing Channel No. 5, a white corset, white stockings, and high heels. Carla looked stunning.

She had told Brad the room number—369, which really amused Carla. He was due to arrive at 7:30, but Carla was ready by 7:00 and was already drinking some champagne.

"Wow!" Micky said. "You look stunning—very sexy indeed."

"Well, I'm expecting a great night, so I thought I would make the extra effort. These are special nights, Micky. We need to make the most of them."

Micky looked cool in his blue jeans and black T-shirt. He was hoping that Brad had been able to get hold of some cocaine, that he'd promised, Micky looks at her, cheers Carla let's have a night to remember, I love my sex party's says Carla, Me too says Micky.

There was a knock at the door. Micky went and answered it. It was Brad.

"I've come with many gifts for you," he joked. He was dressed in a black Hugo Boss suit and a white shirt, looking so handsome.

Carla's eyes lit up. "What would you like to drink, Brad?" she asked.

"JD on the rocks please, Carla."

"You're early," Micky said as he headed for the bathroom.

Carla looked Brad in the eyes. "I hope that's the only time tonight that you come early."

Brad smiled. "You look stunning, Carla, and you won't be disappointed—believe me. I promise.

After about ten minutes, Micky came out of the bathroom to find Carla and Brad laughing and knocking the drinks back. Micky just looked at them.

"Well," said Carla, "I'm a lucky girl tonight. I've got two of the best-looking guys in Vegas, and you're both all mine for the night."

Micky poured himself a brandy. Carla looked like a cat who had a bowl of cream.

"Let's get some of this Colombian love powder on the table," Brad said. He started to put the cocaine on the table and made six lines. They each did a line.

"That feels great," Carla said as she turned and kissed Brad. She started to take his jacket off and unbuttoned his shirt. She could tell he was in good shape.

Brad began to stroke the top of her thighs, while Micky knocked back his brandy and lit a cigar before sitting down to watch the show. Carla kissed Brad's chest, sucking his brown nipples. His dark chest heaved as he grabbed Carla by the arms and threw her down on the bed. He kissed and sucked her nipples, slowly and gently moving down to her stomach. He kissed her stomach and slowly kissed his way down to her thighs. Next, he pulled her underwear down, still kissing her thighs. He moved over and kissed her pussy, slowly licking her up and down, gently kissing and sucking on her pussy. Carla was in heaven. She came within minutes. Carla then grabbed Brad, spun him around, and started to undo his pants. She undressed him and saw his cock was rock hard.

Carla put a line of cocaine on his cock and leaned down to snort it off, sucking him hard and fast at the same time. Brad just laid back and enjoyed the blowjob. Micky soon came over to join in. He took his cock out, and Carla began blowing them both, sucking them hard and fast. She was in wonderland and couldn't get enough.

Micky started to fuck Carla from behind while she blew Brad. Then they swapped, and Brad fucked her hard and deep as she finished Micky off. He came and fell back on the bed. They all did another line, and then Brad grabbed Carla, bent her over the bed, and fucked her hard and fast. Carla reached a massive orgasm. She turned around and threw Brad on the bed before climbing on top of him and fucking him hard.

Brad yelled, "I'm cumming, Carla."

He screamed, and they both came together. Brad begged Carla to stop. She was still fucking him, as she was out of her mind with sex and cocaine. Micky just sat back and smiled. He started laughing, because he'd never seen her like this before.

Micky just carried on, watching the show and sitting there naked with his brandy and cigar. Carla beckoned Micky over and told him to bring some coke with him.

Micky did as he was told, while Carlo got off of Brad. She reclined and put coke all around her nipples, before telling Micky and Brad too suck it off. She loves the feeling of two men at the same time, one on each nipple.

Micky then went down on Carla while she took Brad in her mouth, sucking him hard. Micky then started to fuck her again. All three of them came again and again, all night long. Before long, they were all lying back on the bed, exhausted. The sex had gone on for hours, and Carla loved it. She couldn't get enough. All three of them were lying naked on the bed when Micky woke up a few hours later.

He had been asleep for six hours. He went into the bathroom to shower and shave. It was day five, and he needed to go to work. After half an hour, he came back into the bedroom and found Carla going down on Brad. Micky looked at her.

"Carla, I think you have burnt Brad out. It's time for him to go. It's 7:30, so say your good-byes now."

"Okay, Micky," she said. Carla got up and put her dressing gown on.

Brad put his suit back on, and they say their good-byes.

"Thanks for a memorable night, Carla," Brad whispered.

"Thank you too," said Carla. "You never know …. We might see each other again."

Brad then left.

"Can we do this again with Brad before we go back home, Micky?" Carla asked.

"No," snapped Micky. "Playtime is over now, Carla. It's time to go to work."

CHAPTER 8

DAY FIVE: THE PLAN

It was day five, and Micky was ready to do the job he came to Las Vegas to do.

Micky contacted Mo Green as planned. He needed the information about Vinney Costello's lifestyle so he could put his plan into action. He wanted to know where he lived, where he went drinking, and where he relaxed—everything about him. The plan was to kidnap him and take him out to the Nevada desert and kill him. It was as simple as that.

Later that morning Micky met up with Mo Green as planned, and they talked for a few hours.

"Okay," said Micky. "I'm ready now. Tomorrow I will put my plan into action."

The men had had met for lunch in the Stratosphere hotel. There, they'd had lunch and then gone to the top of the hotel to talk. Micky decided where he was going to snatch Vinney Costello, and everything was ready and planned.

Mo Green was nervous, but Micky was ready to go.

CHAPTER 9

THE SNATCH

On Friday at one o'clock, Vinney Costello locked his office up and left for his Friday sauna and steam room session. He did the same thing every Friday. It was just off the Las Vegas Strip, about a twenty-minute walk from the Flamingo.

Vinney arrived at the sauna and steam room, showed his membership, and walked straight in. He got changed and headed for the sauna. It was quiet—just how Vinney liked it. He sat there just chilling in the sauna, not too busy. It was just right. After half an hour, he headed over for his massage. He passed a guy on the way, and they said hi to each other. Vinney had a good half-hour massage and then headed back toward the steam room. He felt really good, but tired. Vinney sat in the steam room feeling a bit sleepy, very relaxed, and chilled. Suddenly, the door opened, and in walked the man he'd said hi to earlier. The man was tall, dark, and muscular. His black hair was swept back from the cold shower he'd just had, and his white towel was wrapped around his waist. He sat in the corner, but with all the steam in the room, Vinney couldn't see his face. The men said hi to each other again.

"I haven't seen you in here before," Vinney said.

"I haven't been in here before," the man replied.

Still not being able to see his face due to the steam, Vinney introduced himself. "My name's Vinney. I live and work here in Vegas. I come here every week and love it here. It's so relaxing. I just chill out here every Friday after work, but it's quiet today, just how I like it. Do you live and work in Vegas?"

"No," said the man. "I'm here on holiday with my wife."

"I see you're English," Vinney said, surprised. "Whereabouts in England are you from, London?"

"No, not London. I'm here for the gambling. I thought I would try the Flamingo Hotel, just off the Strip. I've heard it's very good."

"That's where I go," Vinney said. "Maybe we can get together and do some tables and have a few drinks afterward, maybe pull some chicks."

"Yeah, why not," the man answered.

Vinney leaned forward and held out his hand. "I never caught your name, my friend."

"Michael," said the man as he leaned forward and out of the steam, revealing his face. "My names Michael, but you can call me Micky."

After a couple of hours in the sauna, Micky suggested showering off and going to the bar area for a few drinks. "Then I will drive us over to the Flamingo, and we can play some tables and maybe get some chicks."

"Great," said Vinney. "We can do some poker or roulette, maybe get some hookers, have some fun. I've got a few contacts over there."

"Okay," said Micky. "Let's get showered."

One hour later, and Micky was at the end of the sauna bar ordering the drinks, while Vinney was chatting with two girls up sitting nearby. He was bragging about going over to the casino.

"You want to join me and my friend and come over to the casino with us?"

"No thanks," said one of the girls. "But if your good-looking friend at the bar wants to come back to our room for a bit of fun with me and my friend, he's welcome."

Vinney laughed. Meanwhile, Micky got the drinks and slipped a Temazepam sleeping pill in Vinney's whiskey. He then waved Vinney over.

"I think those girls are lesbians," Vinney said with a smile. "They didn't like me."

"Never mind them," Micky said. "Here's a toast to our new friendship. Down in one, Vinney."

Vinney knocked the whiskey back in one, and Micky smiled. *That gives me about half an hour to get him to my car*, thought Micky.

"One more," Vinney said.

"Okay, but make it a quick one. I feel lucky today," Micky said.

Vinney brought the drinks over. "Cheers," he said. "Here's to the money we are going to win, and here's to the girls who are going to get laid."

Micky smiled and looked at him as he knocked back his drink.

And to think, the only one who's going to get fucked is you, my fat friend, Micky thought to himself. *I need to get him to the car quickly.* "Come on, Vinney. Let's go."

The two men headed out to the parking lot and over to Micky's car.

"I think those drinks have gone to my head. I feel a bit drunk," Vinney said.

"The fresh air will help," Micky said. "Don't worry and get in the car. That's what you get for drinking with the big boys from England."

Once in the car, Micky looked over at Vinney. His eyes were beginning to droop. *Two more minutes, and he will be out cold.* "Are you okay?" asked Micky.

Vinney didn't reply. Micky looked at Vinney and slapped him across the face a couple of times. *Yep, he's out cold*, he thought. Micky got the cable ties out of the glove compartment and tied Vinney's hands and feet together. When he was done, he gagged him and he put his seat back. He rolled Vinney into the back and onto the floor of the car and then covered him with a sheet.

All done, Micky thought to himself. *Drugged, tied up, covered up, and out cold for a few hours. That's the important bit of the job done. Now I need to contact Carla.*

As agreed, Micky called Carla, who was waiting across the road in a diner. She came straight over and got in the car.

"A couple always looks less suspicious," Micky said.

"You always say that, Micky," Carla told him. She had all the details they gotten from Mo Green as to where and when to meet.

It was Micky's plan to drive out toward the Nevada desert, and for some strange reason that Micky couldn't understand, Mo Green wanted to meet them and be a part of the killing. They had arranged to meet him 180 miles out in the desert at a place called Ma's Diner. It was just off the highway.

Mo Greens knew the area very well, as he went out into the desert most weeks where he liked to camp. Micky thought that was strange, but Mo knew all the old areas and the closed-down old mining towns. Micky reluctantly agreed.

CHAPTER 10

THE DRIVE

Micky and Carla set off out toward the desert. About an hour into the drive, Micky heard Vinney moaning in the back of the car.

"He's starting to come around," Carla said.

Micky pulled the car over to the side of the highway and he checked that there were no cars passing by before asking Carla to look in the glove compartment. She opened it and saw some cloth wrapped up.

"Pass me that," Micky said. He unwrapped the cloth and took out a syringe. "It's heroin, Carla. I got it yesterday from a local dealer. This will knock him out for a good few hours."

Micky got out of the car and walked around to the rear of the car on the inside, away from the road. He opened the car door, grabbed hold of Vinney, and injected him with the heroin, giving him the full amount. He then grabbed Vinney's face and laughed. "Not the trip you expected, is it, my fat friend? This trip will be better. It's not enough to kill you, but it's enough to make you sleep for a few hours."

"What if it kills him, Micky?" Carla asked.

"Then it will save us a job later, won't it?" Micky told her. He then crushed the syringe with his boot and threw the remains into the desert. "No one will trace that," he said before getting back into the car. He smiled at Carla and cleaned his sunglasses. "That will keep him quite for a while, Carla." Micky then sped off down the highway.

"All this is turning me on," Carla said. She then proceeded to go down on Micky while he drove and she gave him a blowjob.

"I love you, babe," Micky said. He then turned the radio up, smiled a cheeky smile, and drove even faster into the desert.

CHAPTER 11

MA'S DINER

A few hours later, Carla and Micky started to approach the agreed meeting place, a small diner just off the highway called Ma's Diner. It was an ideal place to meet, very small, a bit rundown, and out of the way. Micky parked outside the diner and checked on Vinney to make sure he was still out of his head. He was—bound, gagged, and out cold.

Micky looked at Carla and told her he loved her. He then kissed her, and they both headed into the diner. Micky ordered some drinks at the bar, while Carla sat at a table in the corner where it was nice and private. Mo Green hadn't arrived yet, as Micky and Carla arrived early so they could chill out and have a beer.

The woman behind the bar looked to be in her midforties. She was blonde and very slim, wearing a low-cut top that showed off her rather large boobs. She was good looking but was losing her looks and appeared to have enjoyed her life.

"My name's Ma. I'm the owner. I haven't seen you in here before, stranger."

"No. I haven't been in before. Just passing through," Micky said.

"What would you like to eat?" Ma winked and smiled at Micky.

"What do you recommend?" he asked.

"Well, my pussy and nipples are very tasty. If not that, the burgers are my speciality."

"I'll just have the burgers for now, thanks," Micky responded with a smile. "Maybe next time."

"Okay," Ma said. "Maybe next time don't bring your woman."

Micky picked up the beers and went over to sit with Carla. They talked and drank their beers.

Sometime later, Ma brought over the burgers. She leaned over, showing her tits to Micky. There you go, handsome. Enjoy."

One hour later, in walked Mo Green. He looked nervous and edgy, as he sat down next to Carla.

"You want a drink, Mo?" Micky asked.

"Yeah, a double whiskey," he answered.

Micky shouted the drink order to Ma. "You're late, Mo. I don't like people who are late, and I don't even know why you are here," Micky snapped. "Why are you here anyway? You're paying me to do the job, so you don't need to be here."

Carla sat quietly and checked her phone.

"Stop playing on your phone, Carla. We are working," Micky yelled. "Who the hell are you texting anyway?"

"No one, Micky."

Ma brought the whiskey over, giving Micky a sexy wink.

"I'm here, Micky, because I want to see that bastard sleaze ball Vinney Costello get what he deserves," Mo explained, snapping at Micky.

"Okay, let's calm down, Mo," Micky said. "Drink your whiskey. This is the plan … You take us to the spot in the desert that you know, I will kill him and bury him, and then we all go home. It's as simple as that. You got that, Mo?"

"Yes, I've got that," Mo answered.

"It's getting late now," Carla said. "We need to get started."

"How are you going to kill him?" Mo asked.

Micky stared at him. "That's my job, not yours. That's why you're paying me, okay? What have I just said to you?"

"All right," Mo said. "No need to get at me, Micky."

Micky suddenly became angry. "And it's Michael to you. We are working. It's Michael, as in Michael Angelo, as in Michael Caine. Not Micky, you got that? I'm not a fucking mouse."

"He means as in Micky Mouse," Carla added. "Only his friends call him Micky. Ain't that right, babe?

"Yeah, that's right, babe." Micky leaned over and kissed Carla. "I love you, Carla." He then turned to look at Mo and gave him a cold stare that sent shivers down his spine.

Mo suddenly became very scared of his two companions. One minute they were talking about killing someone, and the next minute they were kissing each other and saying how much they loved one another.

"Right," Micky said. "Back down to business. You got the money, Mo?"

"Yes. It's in the car in a suitcase. You can count it if you want."

"Don't worry about that. I will," Micky said. "Okay, let's go now." And with that, they headed out of the diner.

Ma shouted after them. "See you again, handsome. Come back when you've got a better appetite, if you know what I mean." Ma winked at Micky.

Micky winked back and then headed over to the car where Mo showed Micky the money.

"Okay, that's fine. So we will follow you to your hidden desert location," Micky said.

They all got into their cars, and with Mo in the lead, they drove away.

CHAPTER 12

THE DESERT

Micky and Carla followed Mo Green along the highway and on toward the desert. It seems like a never-ending road.

Micky looked at Carla. "If that Mo Green tries to double-cross me, I will kill him too. One more body in the grave won't make much difference. There's something not right about him. Why does he want to be here when he's paying me? It's doesn't add up."

"I agree," Carla said. "He looked nervous and jumpy back at the diner. Let's keep an eye on him. We both need to watch him. By the way, Micky, I think you had a fan back at the diner. I think Ma wanted you to take her around the back and fuck her."

"Yeah, I agree. Maybe we'll call again on the way back, and you can watch. Now turn the radio up. I love this song."

Carla turned the music up. "Light My Fire" by the Doors was playing, and they both sang along as they sped down the highway and into the desert. Carla grabbed two beers from the back seat that she's bought at the diner. She checks on Vinney Costello and slapped him across the face.

"He's still out cold, Micky. Here, have a beer."

They both took a swig of beer. "Cheers, Micky. Here's to the job we are about to do."

"Cheers, Carla. And when it's all done, why don't we go on holiday? Somewhere we can chill and sunbathe and have a few beers and a couple of sex sessions. What about Spain? You love Spain, Carla, don't you?"

"Sounds good to me, Micky. Cheers!" Carla agreed.

Later, Mo Green pulled off the highway and turned down a dirt track. Micky followed him, and they drove for about four miles before turning off again and driving toward some large rocks. Mo pulled over and parked near the rear of the rocks. Micky followed him and pulled up next to him.

"How the hell did he know about this place? It's miles from anywhere," Micky said to Carla.

Mo got out of his car and walked over to Micky's car.

"Where the hell are we?" Micky asked.

"Don't worry. I know the desert very well, I've been coming here for years," Mo said. "It's a long story, but maybe one day I will tell you, Michael."

Micky looked at Carla. His face said it all—he was not happy.

"It's ideal," Carla said. "It's really out of the way … in the middle of nowhere."

"Okay then," Micky said.

Micky and Mo moved the cars so they were facing the rocks. Night was fast approaching, and they needed to use the headlights. Micky got out of the car and looked at Carla, who was on her phone again texting. She finished her text and plugged her phone in to charge.

Micky walked over to the rocks. "We will dig around here, next to the rocks, about four feet down. That should be deep enough for a grave."

"Yes," Mo agreed. "That's great."

Micky looked at him suspiciously.

"Yeah, it looks good," Carla said. As she walked over, she noticed scratch marks on the rocks. "That looks like names that have been scratched on the rocks."

Mo looked at her. "It's probably from hippies who come out here to camp, smoke weed, and have orgies. The dirty bastards."

"Sounds like fun to me," Carla said.

Micky laughed. "You would say that."

"Okay then … So we dig around here then," Mo said.

"Yes," Micky agreed, looking at Mo. "If it makes you feel better, you can dig it." Micky then left to go check on Vinney Costello. "Maybe he can dig his own grave," he muttered as he walked.

Micky opened the car door and dragged Vinney out. He was starting to come to and was mumbling and wriggling, trying to get his hands and feet free. Micky sat him against the rocks and left him there tied and gagged. The horror on his face was evident as he realized what was in store for him.

Mo Green walked over to Vinney, who was trying to say something to Micky through his gag. Mo bent down to Vinney, smiled at him, and hit him in the face.

"This is what you get, Vinney, for double-crossing me." He then kicked him and punched him again.

Micky looked at Mo. "Why the fuck do you really want to be here, Mo?" he asked.

"Because I do," Mo answered. "I'm paying you. I want to see this sleazeball get what he deserves. I will gladly dig the grave and fill it in afterward. How are you going to kill him?"

"I've told you, that's my job," Micky said. "Okay, now let's all calm down now and chill for a while. He walked away and over to Carla.

"Let's have another beer, babe," she said. "We will wait till dark, put the headlights on, dig the grave, kill him, bury him, and then get the fuck out of here."

Micky went over to the car and sat against the wheel. Carla came over to join him and handed him a beer before sitting next to him.

"You're right, Micky. There's something about this guy that doesn't add up. It's like he doesn't trust you. He wants to dig the grave and fill it in afterward, but he's paying you to do all that."

"Like we said, Carla, we need to watch him—both of us. Just keep an eye on him. Let's get the job done and get out of here." Micky looked over at Vinney, who was trying to say something through his gag. Micky just stared back at him.

CHAPTER 13

IT'S MICHAEL, NOT MICKY

As nighttime fell, Micky got a large lamp and shovel out of the back of his car. He rigged the light up and turned on the car's headlights so all the lights were lit and shining on the area where they needed to dig. Carla sat in the car texting but quickly put her phone down when Micky saw her.

"Okay, Mo. I'm ready," Micky said. "We will dig right here. Give me the money now."

Mo walked over to his car, took out the suitcase, and gave it to Micky. Micky opened it and checked before shouting to Carla.

"Can you put that in the car and check it again, babe? I will start digging."

"I want that bastard Vinney to dig his own grave," shouted Mo.

Micky walked over to Mo. "I'll dig it. I'll kill him. I'll fill it in. End of story, and that's it. Then we all go home happy. It's simple. I'm in charge. Okay, Mo?"

"Anything you say. You're in charge, Micky boy."

Micky turned and stared at him.

"Whoops," Carla said.

Micky grabbed Mo around the throat. "What did I say to you?"

Mo smiled and laughed back.

"What did I tell you?! Don't call me Micky!" He lost it and thumped Mo, knocking him down. "I've had enough of you." Micky picked him up and thumped him again. He kicked him again and again, and blood began streaming from Mo's face. "It's Michael, not fucking Micky! How many times do I have to tell you?" Once again, he grabbed him and thumped him. Micky ten kneeled over him and continued thumping him. "It's fucking Michael, as in Michael Jackson." *Thump.* "As in Michael Angelo." *Thump.* "I've told you I'm not a fucking mouse!"

"Yeah!" Carla shouted. "He's not Micky fucking Mouse, you know!"

Micky kept thumping and kicking Mo, who was bleeding badly and half unconscious. Micky hit him one more time and then walked away to try and calm himself down. Vinney Costello was still bound and gagged and was shocked by what he'd just witnessed. Micky sat down next to the car with his head in his hands.

Carla walked over to him. "You never said Michael Caine."

"You what?" Micky said.

"You never said Michael Caine. You always say, 'as in Michael Caine,' when you tell people not to call you Micky."

"Does it really matter? For fuck's sake, Carla."

"I'll do it for you, babe." Carla walked over to Mo Green, who was trying to get up while still bleeding and swollen. She looked down at him and smiled before kicking him in the balls. "As in Michael fucking Caine! You got that, Mo?!"

She then walks back to Micky. "I did it for you, babe. That's because I love you. Now let's calm down and have a beer. Okay, Micky?"

"Thanks, Carla. Love you too. You know what, Carla? You're right." Micky got up and walked over to Mo Green. He leaned in close and said in his best Michael Caine voice, "As in Michael Caine. *Thump.* He hit him again. "And not a lot of people know that." *Thump.* "You got that, Mo?" *Thump.*

Carla looked over and burst out laughing. "Jesus Christ. You're so fucking funny when you're mad, Micky."

CHAPTER 14

THE GRAVE

Micky went back over to the area and started to dig. He looked over at Vinney Costello, who was mumbling and trying to say something. Mo Green was slumped against the car, bloody and bruised.

"Carla, you keep an eye on them two, while I dig this hole," Micky said. He then started digging next to the rocks. After about half an hour of digging, he'd gotten about four feet deep. As he plunged the shovel into the dirt, he came across a shoe. He laughed about it and thought it was a bit strange. Then he found another shoe—old shoes. "Must be those hippies," he said to himself as he carried on digging.

Soon, he started seeing some clothing. That's when he began to realize something was wrong. With the next shovel of dirt, Micky started to unearth a skeleton in an old suit. He noticed a hole in its skull, and as he moved more earth, he came across two more bodies dressed in suits. Three bodies in total, all shot in the head. It was becoming clear to Micky that this was already a grave.

Micky shouted for Mo Green to come over to him. Mo slowly got up and struggled toward him. Mo started to dig with his hands and helped get the three bodies out of the grave. Micky looked over at Carla, who was playing with her phone again.

"Carla, put that fucking phone down. Come here and have a look at this."

Carla quickly joined the men. "Jesus Christ, Micky. What's three bodies doing buried in the desert?"

There were three bodies total—all in suits, old suits—and all had been shot in the head. It was clear all three men had been murdered and buried many years ago. There was also a suitcase lying next to them. They dragged all three bodies out of the grave and then got the suitcase out.

Micky looked at Carla, and they both looked at Mo Green. All three looked at Vinney Costello, who was still trying to say something but was bound and gagged. Mo Green sat down, still shaking from Micky's beating.

"What the fuck do we do now?" Carla asked.

"Let's see if there is any ID on them, not that we can report it," Micky suggested. He started to go through pockets and found some wallets. They all had watches and rings on, so it clearly wasn't a robbery. It was as if they had just been shot and buried.

Micky took the wallet out of the jacket pocket on the first body. It had twenty dollars in it, a photo of a woman and child, and a driver's license, which stated his name was Mr. James Colombo. The next body was identified as Mr. John Rizzo, and the last body was identified as Mr. Frank Lanksky.

Carla and Micky looked at each other. "What the hell have we uncovered here?" Carla asked.

"I don't know," Micky said, "but whatever it is, it's big."

CHAPTER 15

THREE DEAD VEGAS GANGSTERS

1. Big Jim Columbo
2. Johnny Rizzo
3. Frank Lanksky

Mo Green stood up and walked over to the bodies. He turned to Micky. "These three are all famous mobsters who disappeared many years ago. Sometime in the 1940s, all three of them were killed by the mob. Big Jim Colombo was a gangster known for collecting money and dealing with unpaid debts—a killer in his own right. Frank Lanksky was an older guy, a gangster for many years. He was one of Al Capone's men. He lost three fingers in a famous shootout and was known to his friends as Frankie Three Fingers. Johnny Rizzo was an evil gangster known for torturing his victims before he killed them. All three were on Benjamin Bugsy Siegel's payroll—they were his trusted men."

Micky knew that Benjamin Bugsy Siegel, was a gangster who ran Hollywood in the 1940s. He was born in Brooklyn,

New York, in 1906 and was of Jewish American decent. A handsome man with film star looks, he was also an evil psychopath who was the most infamous and feared gangster of his day. He loved women, and the women loved him. He was a very charismatic man who had moved to Hollywood from New York in the 1940s. He had many gangsters working for him. It was his idea to open the first gambling casino/hotel in a small desert town called Las Vegas. He used the mob's money to open the Flamingo Hotel in the Nevada desert. It opened on New Year's Eve 1946, but it was a disaster, and the mob soon got their revenge on Bugsy Siegel for the multimillion-dollar loss. On June 20, 1947, Bugsy Siegel was murdered, shot to death in his girlfriend's house in Beverly Hills. His murder remains unsolved. But little did they know at the time what he had created—it's now the Las Vegas seen today.

Carla was going through the clothes on the dead bodies when she looked over at the suitcase. She went over to it and broke the case open.

"Fuck, Micky. Look at this! There must be a million dollars in here!"

Micky joined her. "Jesus Christ! It's full of money and jewelry."

Carla looked at Micky. "We are fucking rich, Micky. Fucking rich!"

Mo walked over, still wiping the blood from his face. He looked at Micky and Carla and just smiled and walked away. Micky looked over at Vinney Costello, who was still trying to say something through his gagged mouth.

"We need to keep our eyes on those two," Micky said. "Now let's get some rest. It's been a long day. We will sort things out later." Micky gave Carla the suitcase, and she put it with the other suitcase so all of the money was together.

"This has been a crazy day, Micky. I don't think I can take it all in," Carla said.

"It's been a lot to take in," Micky said.

"I've never seen so much money, Micky. We're fucking rich … fucking rich!"

Carla sat in the car, and soon Micky came over to join her. He noticed Carla was on her phone, then charging it, and then checking her messages.

"This isn't the time and place to be checking your messages, Carla."

"I know," she said. "I'm just charging it. You never know when you're going to need it, Micky."

Micky looked at the suitcases on the back seat and then looked over at Vinney Costello, who had fallen asleep. Mo Green leaned against the wheel of his car and was resting.

Micky sat back and shut his eyes. "Let's rest for ten minutes. "Then we will sort things out."

CHAPTER 16

SUNRISE

Micky woke up to the sunrise. He had fallen asleep. He looked at his watch and saw it was 5:30 a.m. He rubbed his eyes and looked around. Carla was asleep in the front seat, and Mo Green was asleep against the car's wheel. Next, he looked at Vinney Costello who was awake. Micky checked the money, as there was well over a million dollars in cash and jewels. He took the suitcases out of the car and put them in the trunk. He stashed the keys in his pocket and looks around. Mo Green had woken up.

Micky grabbed a beer and had a long drink. "That feels better," he said before grabbing another.

Micky walked over to Vinney Costello, who was trying to say something. He grabbed hold of him and stood him up. "You need a beer," Micky said. He took his gag off and gave him a long drink of beer.

Vinney coughed and spluttered and then spit and coughed again. Micky gave him another drink of beer. Vinney drank it all and then looked at Micky. "For fuck's sake. You've got it all wrong, Micky. He's the double-crossing scumbag. He's a lying cheating bastard. We have both been looking for this grave for years."

Micky looked at him, stunned and confused.

"Yes, but I found it first," Mo Green said.

Micky turned around to see Mo Green pointing a gun at them both. He smiled at them both. "The money's all mine now, *Micky*, and the grave will just have a few more bodies in it."

"You fucking scumbag," shouted Vinney.

Bang. Mo shot Vinney in the head, killing him instantly.

"That's him out of the way. Now you, Micky."

CHAPTER 17

THE STORY

"Now let me tell you a story, *Micky*. You see, *Micky* … or is it Michael? No, let's call you *Micky*. You see, a very long time ago, in the 1940s, two gangsters were hired to find and kill those three people who were in the grave. You see, those three guys were on the take, and the mob found out. The Flamingo was a disaster when it first opened. Bugsy Siegel was murdered by the mob, and those three gangsters worked for Bugsy and were draining money from the mob and stashing it away. The gangsters met up with them, killed them, and buried them out here. They put the money in the grave for safekeeping. The plan was to wait for things to calm down for a couple of years and then come back for it. They went back to LA, but soon after that, they turned on each other over the money. Then one night in a bar, they had an argument, and one of the men was shot dead. Are you keeping up with me, Micky?

"The remaining gangster was arrested and charged with murder. He was convicted and sent to prison for life. That is where I met him. You see, Micky … You don't mind me calling you Micky, do you? You see, I did some time in a California state prison. That's where I met him. He was an old man by then, and I got to know him very well. I shared a cell with him, and he used to tell stories about the 1940s gangsters he knew, about how he knew Bugsy Siegel, and about Vegas and the Flamingo. Then, one night he told me about the three gangsters he had killed and the million dollars and jewels in a suitcase, buried in the Nevada desert next to some rocks with their initials scratched on them, so they could find them, and only he knew how to find the grave. He bragged all the time about his good friend Bugsy, how it was his idea to open gambling hotels in Vegas. He talked about the millions of dollars that went missing and how Bugsy eventually paid the price for it, but no one believed him, except me. The old man went into great details about the grave and about everything else. He was too old to care anymore. His life was over, and he had no chance of being released. He knew he would die in prison.

"So when I had done my time and was released from prison, I moved to Las Vegas and settled here. But after a few years of looking for the grave, I couldn't find it. I thought I needed help, but that was my big mistake. I knew Vinney from the local bars and clubs. He knew the desert well. He used to pan for gold and camp out, visiting the old mines out there. So one night after too many drinks, I told him that I needed him. We both looked together and bought old maps, but nothing. Then one day I had the idea that the old gangster had been a bit confused and that he had gotten it slightly wrong, so one day I found it on my own—the scratchings on the rocks, the initials of the dead men. I found the money—it's all mine. But Vinney knew all about it. I don't know how, but he knew I'd found it, so he started ripping me off in business deals, threatening to tell about the money. And so, he had to go.

"You see, Micky, a few more bodies in the grave won't make much difference. It didn't go according to plan. You were supposed to kill him and then go back to England, but now you know about it all. It all went fucking tits up, so you and your crazy fucking girl with the crazy fucking tits need to be killed now. And that's the story, so get down on your knees and put your hands behind your head."

Micky kneeled down and put his hands behind his head. Mo pointed the gun at Micky's head.

"Just one question before I kill you, Micky," Mo said. "Why pencil? I mean, why did I have to text you the word *pencil* for the contact? I thought it was a bit strange."

Micky looked at him. "Well, you see, Mo, a pencil can be removed. It can be erased, rubbed out, taken away, never to be seen again—just like you are going to be." *Thud.* Suddenly, a spade crashed down on Mo's head. He fell to the ground bleeding. Carla had woken up and saw and heard everything.

Micky quickly grabbed the gun. Carla hit him again and again as she screamed, "You bastard! I've got nice tits, not crazy tits."

Micky had seen Carla sneaking up behind Mo Green, so he kept him talking.

Carla continued hitting him and yelling. "Don't call me tits! Don't you dare try to kill my Micky!"

Micky took the spade out of her hands and looked down at Mo. "I think he's dead, Carla. Well done, babe."

Carla was crying with emotion.

"It's okay, Carla. Calm down, babe." Micky bent down and looked at the dead body. He laughed and whispered in Mo Green's ear. "I told you not to call me Micky."

CHAPTER 18

THE CLEANUP

Carla sat against the car smoking a cigarette. Micky walked over and sat with her. He opened two beers, gave one to Carla, and then lit up a cigar and took a long drink of beer.

"What a fucking mess," he said. "Five dead bodies and more than a million dollars. Jesus Christ, Carla. We need to bury the bodies and get the fuck out of here. We will cover are tracks, and it will look like no one's been here and nothing has happened. Okay, babe?"

"Micky, I feel really horny, babe," Carla moaned.

"What?! Fuck me, Carla. Are you not listening? We've got five dead bodies, more than a million dollars in the suitcases in the car, we are in the middle of the desert, and you're feeling fucking horny? Jesus Christ, Carla."

"I'm only saying, babe … I can't help it. There's no need to shout at me," Carla responded.

"Well don't say anything. Let me do the thinking." Micky stood up and looked around. "Let's bury the bodies, clean up, and get the fuck out of here. I've seen enough of this fucking desert."

Micky dragged the bodies over, one by one. First, he dumped Vinney Costello's body in the grave and then Mo Green. He covered them with dirt and then puts the other three gangsters in one by one. Carla was busy at work burning everyone's IDs. After she'd destroyed Mo Green's and Vinney Costello's licenses, she looked at the old IDs from the gangsters. She noticed that Johnny Rizzo had been very cute and tasty when he was young. *If I was around in those days, I would have been his moll. He's right up my alley*, she thought to herself.

Micky looked over at her. "Give it a fucking rest, Carla. For fuck's sake."

She looked at Micky, annoyed. "You're always so grumpy."

Two hours later, Micky had put all the bodies in the grave and buried them. The grave was filled in, and Carla had burnt all the IDs. Micky smoothed everything over so there was no trace of anything. He cleaned the area up, so as not to leave any evidence. When he was done, he looked around and decided it looked perfect—like no one had been here.

Micky looked up at the sky and mopped his brow. Then suddenly—*thud*—Micky was hit by something hard, knocking him out cold.

CHAPTER 19

THE MONEY

Carla had hit Micky over the head with the spade, knocking him to the ground. She leaned over Micky and whispered. "So sorry, babe, you grumpy bastard, but I love the money more than I love you. The money is all mine now."

Carla took the cars keys out of Micky's pocket and went to the car to check on the money in the trunk. She put the money Mo Green had paid Micky into the same suitcase. She took $50,000 out of the case and walked back over to Micky, who was still out cold and bleeding. She put the $50,000 into Micky's pocket. "That will help you a bit, babe. Again, so sorry. Don't come looking for me, because you won't find me." With that, she left Mo Green's car with the keys in it for him and locked the trunk with the money. Carla hopped in the car, sent a quick text, and turned on the radio before speeding off onto the desert path and back onto the highway toward Las Vegas.

One hour later, Carla's phone rang. "Yes. I'm okay," she said. "I will pick you up outside Caesars Palace. I will wait in the parking lot. Bring my clothes and leave the key at the reception desk. You got that, my lover boy? That's my name for you from now on—lover boy. Is that okay?

Carla hung up, pressed her foot down on the gas, turned the radio up, and sped off toward Las Vegas.

CHAPTER 20

THE PICKUP

A few of hours later, Carla arrived back in Las Vegas. She drove down the Strip and approached the Caesars Palace parking lot. She drove in and parked before getting out of the car and lighting up a cigarette. She was still a bit nervous—no, very nervous and still shaking—from what she had just done to Micky. She looked over at the hotel entrance but didn't see anyone there. Carla walked up and down nervously. She then got her mobile phone out and started to dial, but no one was answering. She leaned against the car and waited patiently for twenty minutes, thinking that she needed to clean herself up and have a shower. Then, just as she was about to start to worry and panic, out of the Caesars Palace entrance walked Brad.

Brad walked over to the car, looking cool and handsome. He was six foot two and dark. He was wearing blue jeans and a white linen shirt. His black hair was slicked back, and he was wearing shades.

He's very much like Micky but more fun, thought Carla. He was carrying a bag with his and Carla's clothes in it.

Carla ran over to him and kissed him passionately. After their threesome, Carla had fallen head over heels in lust with him.

They both got in the car. Brad was unaware of what had gone on. He asked Carla, "How did you tell Micky about us?"

"We just fell out and split up," lied Carla. "He's flown back home to England. Don't worry about him, lover boy. He's history. Come and have a look at this, Brad."

They both got out of the car and walked around to the trunk of the car. Carla opened the trunk and showed Brad the case.

"Open it," she said.

Brad opened the suitcase. "Fuck me, Carla. What's all this money?" Brad's eyes lit up.

"Call it my settlement from Micky. He can afford it. He's got loads of money—he's loaded. Well … Where do you want to drive to? I thought we could head out to LA and do some partying."

"Sounds great to me," Brad said. "I've got some family in LA."

They both got in the car and sped off toward the Nevada desert en route to LA. Carla turned the radio up. It blasted out "California Dreamin'."

"I love this song," Carla said. "LA, here we come. Come on, Brad. Let's get to LA and party, party, party."

CHAPTER 21

THE WAKE-UP

Back in the desert, Micky woke up. He was dazed and bleeding. Slowly, he got to his feet and started to stagger around, feeling dizzy and weak. He was trying to make sense of what had just happened. He looked at his watch and realized he'd been knocked out cold for about two hours. He held his head and winced in pain. He looked at his hands and saw he had blood on them. He was bleeding from his head wound. He was still trying to work things out and make sense of what had happened. He went over to the car and leaned on it, not realizing it wasn't his car. He slumped against the car with his head in his hands.

"What the fuck just happened?"

He then started to come round. "Carla!" he shouted. He looked around. "Carla, where are you? Carla, what's happened?" He suddenly realized no one was around. He then remembered burying the bodies. He looked around.

No car, no Carla, and no money, he thought.

Next, he remembered being hit. "Carla, where are you?!" Micky shouted. He felt something in his pocket and pulled a bundle of money out. He stared at it, looked at the ground, and saw the tire tracks from the car where Carla had driven off toward the highway.

"Carla, come on, babe." In that moment, it hit him. "*Shit!* She's gone, the car's gone, the fucking money's gone, everything's fucking gone." He walked over and looked at the desert and into the distance.

"*Carla!*" he screamed.

CHAPTER 22

THE PUZZLE: ONE WEEK LATER

Micky was sitting at the pool area He'd booked himself back into Caesars Palace hotel, his head is still hurting from the knockout blow that Carla had given him. He needed six stitches to close the wound in the back off his head, and he was still having bad headaches. He sat there sunning himself in his Bermuda shorts, trying to work the puzzle out.

Thoughts ran quickly through his head. *What happened and why? What motive would Carla have for betraying me? Her mobile phone is dead, so she must have changed phones. It doesn't make sense. She left me dying in the desert. She took all the money—more than a million dollars. She must have gone back to England. Where else would she go? I wonder if Brad as seen her about.*

Micky went over to one of the waiters and asked about Brad. No one had seen him or heard anything, so Micky went inside and asked at the front desk if anyone had seen him.

"He handed his notice in and left," the woman behind the desk told him. "Maybe he started a new job with better money."

"Yeah," Micky said, not thinking anything of it. He went back to the pool to sunbathe.

Micky combed back his dark black hair, put his shades on, threw on a tight white T-shirt on, and went over to the pool bar. "Give me a cold beer," he said.

The guy behind the bar handed Micky a cold beer. "That'll be three dollars. You going to the show tonight?"

"No," Micky said. "Just a quiet night at the lounge bar for me. Who's on?"

"It's a burlesque drag show—loads of beautiful girls/boys for you, if you know what I mean. You can't tell the difference, Micky," the barman said.

"Yeah, that might be good," Micky said. "What's your name?"

"Tommy," answered the barman.

"Are you going to the show when your shift is finished?"

"No, not me," Tommy said. "I'm going on holiday next week, so I'm going to look at some rental cars. I'll be driving up to Santa Barbara with my wife."

"Sounds fun," Micky said. "Have a good time, buddy." Micky left the bar and headed over to a table where he sat down and took a long drink.

Rental car … That's it. What happened to the car we rented? he thought to himself. *Carla hired the car for the whole trip. She must have taken it back, or the police would be after her. I need to go around to the car showrooms and see if it's been returned.*

Micky decided to head back to his hotel room where he showered and changed clothes. As soon as he was done, he headed down to the front desk and asked the hotel doorman to order him a cab. When the cab arrived, Micky jumped in it and gave the guy the showroom address. Five minutes later, the cab arrived at the showroom. Micky jumped out and told the driver to wait for him. He then made his way to the reception area, where he was greeted by a pretty, young, dark-haired receptionist. Micky explained about Carla coming in and renting a Mustang for a few days. He gave her the details about Carla and the car.

"I can't really give information about clients," the receptionist said.

Micky looked at her. "She's my sister, you see, and I want to surprise her. I've just arrived this week. I'll make it worth your while." Micky then pulled out a one-hundred-dollar bill. He smiled and leaned forward with the bill.

The woman looked into his eyes. "Okay then," she said. "She's rented it for another two weeks. Said she was going to LA and that she was dropping it off at one of our showrooms. But hang on … She extended it. She called from Palm Springs to say that they were chilling out for a week there and then going to LA."

"Did she leave a contact number?" Micky asked.

"Yes, she did … Here you are." She wrote the mobile number down for Micky.

"Thanks." Micky entered the mobile number into his phone and gave the woman a big kiss and one hundred dollars.

"She's got another few days left on the car rental," the girl said.

"What's your rental drop-off point address in LA?" Micky asked.

The woman wrote it down for him.

"Thanks for this. My sister will be surprised when she sees me." Micky walked out of the showroom and toward the cab. He stopped dead in his tracks. "She said *they* … She said *they* were chilling out." Micky turned around and walked back over to the receptionist.

"Excuse me," Micky said. "Can I ask you just one more thing?"

"Only if you take me out for a drink tonight," the woman responded.

"You said *they* are staying in Palm Springs chilling out."

"Yes. When she came in the showroom, her boyfriend was with her. They were holding hands and kissing."

"What did he look like?" Micky asked.

"He was tall, dark-skinned, handsome, but not as handsome as you … not as hunky or as mysterious either."

Micky was puzzled. *Who the fuck does Carla know out here in Las Vegas?*

"So what about my drink tonight?" she asked.

"I think you deserve one after that. I'm staying at Caesars Palace hotel. Let's meet in the lounge bar around eight o'clock." Micky turned and started to walk out.

The woman called after him. "Are you not picking me up?"

"Eight o'clock," shouted Micky. "And don't be late. He jumped in the cab and told the driver to take him back to the hotel.

Once back at the hotel room, Micky lay on his bed, puzzled. "Who is this fucking boyfriend?"

CHAPTER 23

THE RECEPTIONIST

At 7:50 p.m. at Caesars Palace lounge bar, the elevator opened, and out walked Micky, wearing a blue suit with a white Armani shirt opened at the neck. He looked stunningly handsome—cool and rugged. He had three days' worth of black stubble on his face, and his dark hair was swept back. He headed over to the bar and found an open barstool. Micky ordered a whiskey sour on the rocks and then looked at his watch. He was early—he was always early, because he hated being late.

Micky heard a voice behind him. "Hi there, mystery man."

Micky turned around to see the receptionist standing there. "Hi," he said as he stood up to greet her. He pulled a barstool out for her. "You look stunning."

"Thank you. You're a gentleman. Nobody's ever pulled a chair out for me before."

Micky looked her over and thought she looked beautiful in her white DKNY halter dress with her dark, flowing hair.

"So what's your name?" the woman asked. She thought it was sexy and mysterious to have a date with a handsome man without even knowing his name.

Micky smiled at her. "My name is Michael, but you can call me Micky. And your name is?"

"Eva. My name is Eva. I'm twenty-eight years old, and I was born and brought up in New York. I came to Las Vegas three years ago after a breakup with my boyfriend at the time, and I love it here. But the job's a bit boring, apart from today when you came in."

"What would you like to drink?" Micky asked.

"I think I'll have a glass of white wine please."

Micky ordered the wine, and the two chatted and laughed for a couple of hours.

"You haven't told me what you do for a job," Eva noted.

Micky looked her in the eyes before answering. "I'm in the business of solving people's problems."

"What sort of job is that?" she asked.

"It's just business—a bit boring. I travel a lot," Micky said. Wanting to change the subject, he stood up. "Let's drink up, and we will go and have a few more drinks in the casino."

He helped Eva off her barstool, and they headed over to the hotel casino.

"Have you played before?" Micky asked.

"Only a little bit when I'm out with the girls," Eva answered.

After a few hours of playing the tables and drinking, the pair headed over to the casino bar. Eva was slightly drunk and giggling. Micky asked her if she thought Carla was still in Palm Springs or LA.

"I would say Palm Springs, then up to LA to drop the car off. If I were you, Micky, I would go to Palm Springs first, but how would you find her?"

"I don't know," Micky admitted.

"Well, when I met Carla, she was wearing designer gear from head to foot. She looked like she has money, so if I were you, I would head for the expensive hotels like the Ritz-Carlton on Frank Sinatra Drive, or maybe the Hilton. I'll tell you what I will do … I will call her tomorrow and say that we need a contact address for the car rental, then I will text you and let you know the address. Then you'll be able to surprise your sister."

"That would be great," Micky said, "absolutely brilliant. She will be so surprised. I can't wait to see her face."

Eva looked at Micky. "Do I get a reward for being such a good girl for you?"

"You certainly do," he said. "You certainly do. If you don't mind me saying, why don't we go to my room for a nightcap or something else a bit stronger maybe."

*****

The next morning at 7:00, the alarm went off. Micky woke up and switched it off. He looked over at Eva, who was lying next to him sleeping. She was tired out after a night of passion with Micky.

Micky got up and headed to the bathroom to shave and shower. When he was done, he went back into the bedroom with just a white towel around his waist. He leaned over and kissed Eva.

"Wake up, sleepy head," he whispered.

Eva woke up and kissed him as she tried to drag him back into bed. "You look and smell so sexy, Micky. Get back in bed."

"No," Micky said. "I'm checking out this morning, and you have to work at nine o'clock. You jump in the shower, and then when I've checked out, I'll drop you off at work."

By 8:15, Micky was checking out. The pair walked out of the hotel and got into Micky's rental car. Micky drove Eva to work.

"You're going to look a bit odd going in work in your white DKNY halter dress," he said.

Eva just laughed. "Will I see you again, Micky?"

"Yeah. You've got my number. We will meet up again when I come back to Vegas." He kissed her and said good-bye. "And don't forget to send the address to me." Micky then drove off and headed out of Vegas and straight toward Palm Springs.

CHAPTER 24

PALM SPRINGS

After two hours of driving on the highway, Micky remembered the diner where he'd met Mo Green. He looked for the sign at the roadside. A few minutes later, it appeared over the horizon: Ma's Diner. *That's the one*, he thought to himself. He decides to drop in and see if Carla had been there, so he turned off the highway and drove toward the diner.

It was quiet inside, and Micky found Ma behind the bar.

"Well, handsome, I never thought I would see you again," Ma said. "What can I get you?"

"Just a coffee please," Micky said as he sat at the bar.

"Are you on your own this time," Ma asked.

"Yes, I am. Do you remember the last time I came in I was with someone? A girl."

"Yeah," Ma said. "I remember. Nice tits."

"You seen her since?" Micky asked.

"Yeah, she came in about a week ago with a cute guy— very nice. He was hot, really hot, but they drank up and left."

"Okay," said Micky. "Did this guy have a name?"

"No. I just called him cute ass."

"All right," said Micky. "I know I'm on the right track. Thanks for that." He finished drinking his coffee in silence and then looked back at Ma. "I'm off now. Thanks, Ma."

"You're not stopping for your supper?" Ma said, winking and pushing her tits out.

"No. Maybe on the way back, but thanks for the offer." Micky left and got back in his car to continue his drive toward Palm Springs.

After another hot two-hour drive, Micky arrived in Palm Springs. He headed straight for the center of town and stopped at the first decent hotel he saw. Micky approached the front desk to ask about the hotel and then checked in. Micky headed straight to his room where he started to unpack before taking a shower to freshen up. Micky decided to lay on the bed for an hour to chill out. After resting, he changed into some clean clothes. Feeling fresh and clean, he checked the time—3:30 p.m. Micky checked his phone but had no messages. He made his way down to the front desk to ask about any local restaurants where he could get something to eat.

"You can eat in the hotel restaurant," the clerk told him. "It's Italian."

Italian was Micky's favorite, so he went in and sat down. He ordered a meal and a bottle of Italian Chianti.

After his meal, Micky sat in the hotel lounge to drink his wine. He decided to send Eva a text.

"Did you find out where Carla is staying?"

The reply came back within minutes: "No. She hasn't gotten back to me yet. Where's my kiss on my text, mystery man?"

Micky didn't reply. He was ready for business. He looked at Carla's number in his phone, wondering whether he should to text her but decided against it. He didn't want to warn her. *Anyway, she thinks I'm half dead somewhere in the desert*, Micky thought to himself.

Instead, Micky just sat in the lounge, drinking and thinking about the five bodies in the grave back in the desert—Mo Green, Vinney Costello, and those three old gangsters. *I might have to put another couple in.*

A few hours later, Micky received a text. It was from Eva: "Carla is stopping at a Palm Springs hotel, 701 Canyon Drive, Palm Springs. She just got back to me."

Micky texted back: "Brilliant." Micky checked his watch and realized it was getting late, so he decided to get an early start in the morning. *Carla will be surprised—very surprised—when she's sees me*, he thought with a chuckle before heading back to his hotel room for an early night.

The next morning Micky was up at 7:30. He showered but decided to skip shaving and leave his dark stubble. He put on his blue jeans and a black T-shirt and headed down to the restaurant for breakfast. He was in a good mood. He knew where Carla was, and, just as important, he knew where the money was. He ordered a full breakfast with coffee and flirted with the waitresses, laughing and joking with them. He ordered more food and more coffee. "I need to keep my strength up for today," he joked.

"You have a busy day, sir?" asked the waitress.

"I certainly do," Micky said. "It should be a very interesting day."

Micky finished his breakfast and left the restaurant. He passed the hotel shop on the way out and bought a blue baseball cap. He put it on, along with his shades, and then headed over to his car. After entering the hotel address in his GPS, Micky set off.

Sometime later, Micky arrived at the Palm Springs hotel where Carla was staying. He drove up, parked next to the hotel, and walked inside. He walked straight to the front desk to speak to the man working.

"I'm thinking of stopping here," said Micky. "Could you give me some idea of the room prices?"

"Certainly," said the man as he handed Micky some paperwork.

"It looks good. Could I take a look around?" Micky asked.

"Of course you can. Feel free to look around." he pointed Micky toward the pool area and restaurant.

Once the man walked off, Micky was free to look around on his own. He looked in the breakfast lounge, but she wasn't there. He knew Carla and was sure she was either sunbathing or shopping, so he headed out to the pool area and ordered a drink. He made himself comfortable in a shaded corner. With his baseball cap and shades, unshaven face, and T-shirt and jeans, he didn't draw any attention to himself.

Micky sat in the shade overlooking the pool area so he could see who was coming and going. He'd been sitting there drinking coffee for an hour and a half when he ordered another drink. He was willing to wait there all day if he had to. Then, he saw her.

Carla walked out on to the pool area wearing a dress and carrying a shoulder bag. She looked like she was going shopping. She walked over to the sun bathing area, sat down next to a man, and kissed him. Micky tried to make out who the man was but couldn't quite tell. He didn't recognize him. The man was wearing a sun hat. Carla spoke to him for five minutes and then got up and left. Micky really wanted to know who the man was, but he need to follow Carla. Micky paid for his drinks in anticipation of Carla leaving.

Carla set off walking out of the hotel and headed toward the shops. She walked, as the shops were nearby. Micky followed her, keeping his distance but staying with her in and out of the shops. Carla did not realize she was being followed. After a while, Carla stopped at a cocktail bar for a drink and ordered herself a cocktail. She then sat outside in the shade with her sunglasses on.

Micky sat in a bar across the road, drinking a beer and watching her. He laughed and thought about how he could get his revenge. He watched her like a hawk. Micky looked at his watch and then at his phone. *Now it's time for some games*, he thought to himself. Micky sat at the bar, smiling.

Carla sipped her cocktail and flirted with the bar staff. He heard her phone signal she'd gotten a new text message. She picked her phone up and looked at the text. It read: "PENCIL." *Fucking shit. It's Micky.*

Carla was stunned. *How does Micky know my new number?* She knocked her drink over, as she'd become a bundle of nerves. The waiter came over to help her and he cleaned up her table. "Are you all right?" he asked.

"Yes," she replied. "I've just gotten some bad news, that's all." She sat there thinking about what the text meant.

The waiter brought her another drink. "Do you need anything else, miss?" the waiter asked.

"No thanks. I'll be okay." She calmed herself down and took a long drink. *It can't be that bad*, she thinks. *He doesn't know where I am.* Her phone went off again. She looks at the text.

It read: "Hope you're enjoying Palm Springs. Is your cocktail nice?"

"Fuck me," Carla said as she jumped up. "He's here!" She paid for her drinks and set off in a hurry back to the hotel. Carla was in a panic. She knew Micky and knew his temper.

CHAPTER 25

MICKY'S HERE

Back the hotel, Carla rushed into the pool area and found Brad still sunbathing.

"Brad, wake up. Wake up." She shook him. "Brad, fucking wake up! Brad, sits up."

"What's wrong?" he asked.

"It's Micky. He's here in Palm Springs. We need to leave!"

"Why?" asked Brad.

"Because we do. Don't ask questions. Let's go back to our room and pack and then get the fuck out of here. We can head to LA."

"But what's the problem? He's only an ex-boyfriend. I imagine you have loads of ex-boyfriends."

"Look, Brad. I'm leaving. Either come with me or stay here, but I'm fucking leaving. Okay?"

"Well, okay," Brad said. He looked at Carla, who was clearly in a panic. "But I don't understand why. He's only an ex-boyfriend."

They both headed back into the hotel and toward the elevator so they could go up to the room and pack their bags. Brad was still puzzled.

"I thought he'd gone back to England," Brad said.

"So did I," Carla said. Carla was furiously packing her suitcase and decided to call down to the front desk to order a bellboy to come up for their luggage.

"Why are you so frightened of Micky?" Brad asked.

Carla snapped back at him. "Just fucking pack your suitcase or fucking stop here. It's up to you, but I'm off."

"I think there's is something you're not telling me, Carla. You and Micky were boyfriend and girlfriend, you came out to Vegas for a vacation, you didn't get along, and you had a falling out and split up. What's the problem? I've never asked any questions about the money. I don't get it, Carla."

Carla stared at Brad. You will get it if you don't fucking pack your case, believe me. You don't know Micky. Now shut the fuck up and pack."

Brad stared at her and then started packing his case.

Suddenly, there was a knock at the door.

"Get that," Carla said. "It will be the bellboy for our luggage."

Brad went over and opened the door. There stood Micky. Brad was stunned. Micky stood there pointing a gun at his head.

"Well, well, well … If it isn't Brad the shag. I wondered who the guy was. You must have been good in bed. She never bothers about her vacation shags again." He looked over at Carla. "Hello, Carla. Long time, no see. You look really good. It must be all that desert sun or … I almost forgot … all that money. I think we need to talk, don't you? Now sit down, Carla."

Micky looked at Brad. "And you, fuck face. Be a good little boy and pour me a brandy. Make it a double with two ice cubes, and I think you better make Carla one. She's going to need it. This is going to be a long, long chat. Isn't it, Carla?"

Sipping his brandy, Micky pointed the gun at Brad. "You can leave, Brad. This doesn't really concern you. You're free to go."

Brad looked at Micky. "I'm not leaving without Carla."

Micky walked over to Brad and got right up in his face, nose to nose. "You see what it is, Brad the shag. Carla's going nowhere. You got that? Now go and sit the fuck down and keep quiet." Micky put the gun away and looked over at Carla. "Carla, let's talk."

Carla sat there shaking.

"I've got three questions to ask you," Micky said. "Number one, why did you do it? Number two, where's the suitcase full of money? Number three, why him? You can take your time, Carla. We've got plenty of it—all night if needed."

Suddenly, there was a knock at the door. Carla jumped up and ran to the door. Micky quickly followed her.

Carla answered the door. It was the bellboy for the cases. Micky appeared alongside her.

"We won't be needing you, thank you. We've decided to stay on another couple of days. Haven't we, guys?"

Carla agreed and closed the door. Micky ordered her to sit down. She looked at Micky, still shaking.

"I'll tell you what I'll do, Micky. I will give you half the money. If you kill me, you will get nothing. You see, the money is in safe-deposit box, and only I know where it is—not Brad, not you, Micky, just me. So, you see, I'm holding the cards. If you want half a million dollars, then you let us go, or you will get nothing."

Brad looked at her. "This is crazy. What the fuck is going on? I don't understand."

Carla looked at him. "Just keep quiet, Brad. You're out of your league."

Micky paced up and down, thinking for a few minutes. He stopped to look at Carla. "When can you get the money?"

"Tomorrow," she said.

"Let me think." Micky said. "So how do I know you won't run?"

"We won't. I promise, Micky," Carla said. "I got greedy last time."

Brad jumped up. "Hang on, Micky. Why should Carla give you any money?"

Micky grabbed him and hit him hard, knocking him down. I told you to sit down and be quiet." He hit him again. "And don't call me Micky. It's Michael to you from now on. You got that, shag face?"

Carla dragged Micky away from Brad. "Leave him alone." He doesn't know anything. Go and have a beer, Brad, while I talk to Micky."

"No," Brad said. "I'm not leaving you alone with that crazy bastard, Carla."

"Well let's all go down and have a beer in the bar," Carla suggested. "We are not going to sort anything out like this, Micky."

Brad picked himself up and walked to the bathroom to wash his face.

"Let's sort this out like adults," Carla said.

Micky laughed and looked at Carla. "Okay," he said. "But nothing funny, Carla. Remember what happened in the desert. I've got a lot on you. Remember what happened too Mo Green."

They all got ready, and Micky looked at Brad. "You can stay here, Brad. This doesn't concern you."

"I'm not leaving Carla with you on her own. I've told you. You're crazy."

Micky laughed and put the gun away. He got up in Brad's face and smiled. "You ain't seen nothing yet, fuck face."

The three of them left the hotel room together and headed down to one of the hotel bars. Micky smiled at Carla while keeping a close eye on both of them.

They all entered the lounge bar and headed straight over to the corner of the lounge where it was quiet. They sat down at a table, and Brad ordered drinks. Moments later, the drinks arrived, and everyone took a large drink and ordered a second round.

"Right," Brad said. "I'm the innocent one here. I don't know what's gone on."

"Shut the fuck up, Brad."

"No, Michael. I won't. This needs sorting out. If you two can't sort it, I will. Carla is the only one who knows where the money is, so she's right. She is holding the cards." Brad thought for a moment. "So if this is all right with you, Michael, I will make sure that Carla brings the money to the hotel tomorrow at lunchtime. We'll meet you in our room, and she'll split the money with you. Then everyone' goes home happy. Okay? … Answer me Michael. Please."

"How do I know you won't disappear with the money?" Micky asked.

"You've got my word, Michael. I promise. You can trust me. I will make sure the money is in the hotel room tomorrow at lunchtime. Is that all right, Carla?"

She looked at Brad and Micky and nodded her head in agreement.

"Let's put an end to this," Brad said, holding out his hand.

Micky shook his hand. "You've got an honest face, Brad. But if you let me down, I will find you, and I will kill you. You got that? Do you understand, Brad?"

"I understand. But don't worry. The money will be here tomorrow at lunchtime. Won't it, Carla?"

"Yes, it will," Carla agreed, looking at Micky. "I'm so sorry, Micky. I just got greedy."

Brad stood up and looked at them both. "I need to go to the bathroom. I'll let you two talk for a while?" He then got up and left for the bathroom.

Micky leaned forward and looked at Carla. "Why did you do it, Carla? We had all that money, we had a good life, we were good together."

"I'm so sorry. I got greedy, Micky. I'm sorry. We all make mistakes, and I realize now it was wrong. Seeing you again makes me realize how much I loved you. You're right—we were good together. When you shouted and hit Brad back at the room, you looked so sexy. It turned me on,"

Micky laughed. "You never change, do you, Carla?"

"Let's keep the money—me and you, Micky—and get rid of him. He's boring—not as much fun as you. We all makes mistakes … Come on, Micky."

Micky looked at her.

"Come on, Micky … Me and you, together again. Forgive me. I'll make it up to you, I promise."

"I don't know." Micky said.

"Look," Carla said. "I will have the money back at the room by lunchtime tomorrow as planned, and then we can just leave with it. It's ours anyway, not his."

"But what if he goes to the police?" Micky asked.

"He won't," Carla said. "I will say he raped me. I think it carries a life sentence out here … Look, he's coming back now. Please think about it, Micky. Tomorrow, lunch back at the room, a million dollars, me and you back together again."

"Okay, Carla. I will think about it tonight."

Just then, Brad came back to the table. "Okay, I'll agree to arrange a meeting with you both tomorrow at noon in your room. Don't let me down, Brad. You either, Carla, or next time I won't be so friendly."

"We won't let you down. You've got my word, Michael, and I always keep my word," Brad said. "I will be there with the money—me and Carla at noon, in our room."

"That rhymes," Carla said, smiling.

Micky glared at her. "Okay then."

"Me too," Carla said. "I'll be waiting for you tomorrow, Micky."

"And remember what we talked about, Carla," Micky said.

Brad and Carla left and headed back to their room, leaving Micky in the bar lounge. Micky watched them leave and smiled to himself. He was thinking that maybe Carla did deserve a second chance. He laughed and walked over to the bar. Thinking about what Carla said, he ordered a brandy and sat down, smiling. He was thinking about the money and maybe hooking up with Carla again. *I must admit*, thought Micky, *she is good fun to be with. I've missed her in a strange way.* He drank up and headed out of the hotel.

Micky headed back over to his car, opened the car door, and looked up at the hotel. He smiled to himself and leaned back against the hood of the car. Micky then took out a cigar, lit up, and took a few puffs. He looked up at their hotel balcony and saw Carla looking down at him. Micky smiled and waved at her, as if to say, "I'm watching you, Carla. I'm watching you."

I hope those two don't stitch me up, thinks Micky, *because if they do, I'll kill them both.*

He looked at his watch. It was eight o'clock and starting to get dark. It had been a long day, so Micky got back into his car and headed back to his hotel.

CHAPTER 26

MY NAME'S GLORIA

Back at his hotel, Micky shaved and showered and generally cleaned himself up. He was in a good mood and singing. He'd found Carla and was confident of getting his money back—and also maybe getting back together with Carla. She was crazy but fun.

I think maybe I could forgive her, Micky thought to himself. He put on his blue suit, white Armani shirt, and brown shoes. He combed his black hair back and slicked it down with a touch of gel. He holstered his gun and clipped it to his pants, so he could tuck it away, hiding it under his jacket. When he was all ready to go, Micky looked at himself in the mirror.

"You still got it, Micky," he said to himself. "Maybe when I get my money, I'll head up to LA, Hollywood, and be a film star. He quickly pulled the gun out and pointed it at the mirror. "You talking to me, Micky? I said: You talking to me?"

Micky laughed at himself. He loved Robert De Niro films and liked his impression of him, even if no one else did. He left the room and headed down to the bar lounge. It was eleven o'clock at night, and he was ready to drink a few beers, and maybe get lucky with some good-looking young chick. He headed over to the bar and ordered a drink.

"A large, cold beer please," he said as he sat at the bar. He smiled and said good evening to the couples around the bar. He was on the prowl and feeling lucky. *There must be an attractive woman out there who wants my body tonight*, he thought. Then saw a beautiful blonde smiling at him. She was sitting on her own in the corner of the bar lounge, so Micky smiled back. "I think you still got it, Micky baby," he mumbled to himself.

Micky shouted over to the waiter. "Hey, buddy. What's that leggy blonde beauty drinking over there?"

"Which leggy blonde beauty?" asked the waiter.

"Over there, sitting on her own," Micky said, pointing in the blonde's direction.

The waiter looked at Micky. "Oh! *Her.* Right … er … white wine I think. Yes, it's white wine."

"Okay," Micky said. "Send her a white wine over from me. Put it on my tab. In fact, make it a large white wine. I feel lucky."

The waiter smiled at Micky. "Anything you say, buddy."

Micky smiled over at the blonde and raised his glass. She smiled back and raised her glass. The waiter poured the wine and took it over to her. She looked at Micky and waved him over. He picked his drink up and winked at the waiter before heading over to her table.

"Hello. I'm Micky. And your name is?"

"My name's Gloria," she answered. "Thank you for the wine."

"It's my pleasure," Micky said. "Can I sit down?"

"Yes, of course you can. Anyone who buys me a large glass of wine can sit with me all night. The men nearly always buy me a beer," she said with a laugh.

Micky laughed. "Beer? Well you must be keeping the wrong company, Gloria."

She laughed again. "That's a matter of opinion, Micky."

They both started laughing. The waiter looked over and laughed too. Micky sat down and chatted the night away, hour after hour, beer after beer, wine after wine, laughing and joking and flirting.

"This is such fun," Gloria said.

"Well," Micky said, "it's getting late. If you want to come back to my room for a little fun and wine, I'm up for it."

"Why not?" Gloria said. "It's been a long time since a man asked me back to his room. It should be fun, Micky, and I've got a nice big surprise for you."

"Okay. Can't wait—sounds like fun to me. Listen, Gloria. I'll just go to the bathroom and freshen up. Maybe get some condoms? And then I will sign for the drinks, and we can go have some sexy fun. I'll be two minutes."

"Don't be long, big boy."

Micky smiled. "I won't be, my little cutie."

Micky headed over to the bar to sign for the drinks.

"Have you had a good night, Micky?" the waiter asked.

"Yes," Micky said, "and it's not over yet. She's coming back to my room for some sexy fun. I've still got the looks, buddy, I can still pull 'em."

"Yes, you certainly can, Micky," the waiter said.

Micky headed for the bathroom. A few moments later, while Micky was washing his hands, the waiter came in.

"Listen, Micky, I need to tell you something," the waiter said.

"What is it? Are the drinks free?" Micky asked with a laugh.

"No, it's not that." The waiter looked Micky straight in the eyes. "She's a man."

Micky looked at him, confused. "What do you mean she's a man? Who is?"

"Gloria is. She's a man," the waiter repeated.

Micky laughed. "Don't talk so fucking crazy. Don't you think I would have noticed? It's Micky you're talking to."

"Micky, I can't let you do this."

"Do what?" Micky asked.

"Look," the waiter said. "She's a chick with a dick. She's a cock in a frock. She's a Bob with a knob. She's a fucking guy, Micky. He's a Vegas drag queen from downtown Palm Springs."

Micky just stood there looking at him. He was stunned into silence. Micky didn't speak for a couple of minutes and then looked at the waiter. "I thought she had big feet."

At that moment, the door flung open. It was Gloria. She was standing there looking sexy and gorgeous in her glamorous dress. She looked at Micky, and Micky stared at her feet and then her hands.

"Hey, Micky, my sweetheart. Are you cheating on me, or do you want me to shake it for you?" laughed Gloria.

Micky flipped, grabbed her by the scruff of the neck, and pinned her against the wall. He pulls his gun out and pressed it against her groin. "I've a good mind to blow your cock off."

Gloria smiled. "Now there's an offer I can't refuse."

"I meant with the fucking gun," screamed Micky.

The waiter grabbed Micky. "Come on, calm down, Micky. It's just a mistake. You've had a few drinks and made a mistake. Let her go."

"*Her?* It's a fucking guy," shouted Micky. He then pulled her wig off. "See."

"Come on, let go of her before someone comes in here and calls the cops."

"Yeah, okay," Micky said. "You're right." Thinking of Carla and the money, he threw Gloria against the wall and pointed at her. "Now get the fuck away from me."

Gloria put her wig back on and tidied herself up. "You've broke my fucking heel," she said.

"I'll break your fucking neck if you come near me again. Now go," shouted Micky.

Gloria opened the door, looked at Micky, and said, "You know, you shouldn't knock it till you've tried it." With that, she left.

The waiter looked at Micky. "It's time for bed, Micky."

"I should have listened to my dad," Micky said. "He always used to say, never marry a women with big hands."

"Why's that," asked the waiter.

"Because they make your cock look small," Micky said. He looked at the waiter. "I think you're right, buddy. It's time for bed."

CHAPTER 27

THE ARRANGEMENT

The alarm went off, and Micky woke up. He looked at his phone for the time and saw it was nine o'clock, time to get up. He shaved and then jumped in the shower and started to remember what happened the night before. He smiled to himself. *I suppose it could have been worse if I would have brought her back here.*

Micky showered and dried off and then puts on his blue jeans and a black T-shirt. He clipped his holster on to his belt and puts the gun in it. He puts his Armani watch on, sprayed himself with cologne, and then put on his black bomber jacket to hide the gun. He slipped on his converse trainers, combed his black hair back, and put his shades on. Now he was ready to go.

Let's hope Carla and Brad are there and have kept their side of the arrangement, he thought to himself. *And I hope they have brought the money. If not, I will kill them both.*

Micky headed down to his car, got in it, and drove off toward Carla and Brad's hotel. After a ten-minute drive, he arrived at the hotel and immediately looked to see if Carla's car was still there. He drove over and parked across from her car. Micky got out, lit a cigar, and leaned against the car. He looked up at Carla's balcony.

There wasn't any sign of activity, but he wasn't concerned. They both knew that he meant business. Just then, he saw Brad opening the balcony doors. He smiled and waved at Brad, but he just got a stare back. Micky just laughed. He knew he understood everything now. Micky locked up the car and walked into the hotel. He looked at his watch. It was eleven o'clock. He was a bit early, so he bought a coffee and a sandwich at the bar and sat there for an hour.

When noon hit, it was time to go to the room, so Micky headed over to the elevator. He went up to the second floor, walked down the hall to the hotel room, knocked at the door, and waited. There was no answer. He knocked again louder and then again even louder.

Finally, Brad answered the door. "Okay, I heard you," Brad said. "I was in the bathroom."

Micky walked in, smiling. "Hello, Carla. Carla?! Hello, Carla?" He looked around for Carla and the money but didn't see either. He looked at Brad. "Where's Carla, and where's the money?? Micky pulled his gun out and pointed it at Brad.

"It's okay. Don't worry. She was just called out for something," Brad explained.

"Like what?" Micky said.

"I don't know … some woman thing. She will be back soon."

"Where's the money?" Micky asked again.

"Put the gun down, Micky. The money's here."

"Where's the money? I won't ask again."

"It's locked up in the wardrobe," Brad told him.

Micky started to panic. "Where is she?" He pointed the gun in Brad's face. "Open the fucking wardrobe now, or I'll kill you."

"Look. Chill out, Micky and have a beer." Brad started to open the wardrobe when Carla walked in.

"Where have you been?" snapped Micky.

"I just called out for some makeup," she answered.

"I told you, Micky," Brad said as he threw the old suitcase full of money on the bed.

Micky opened the suitcase.

"All the money is there. Now relax, Micky," Carla said.

Brad opened three bottles of beer and gave one to Carla and one to Micky. "Now relax, have a beer, and chill out. Calm down. It's sorted. Okay, Micky?"

Micky smiled. "Okay then. You had me worried." He drank his beer in one big gulp.

"I've kept my part of the bargain," Carla said. "What about yours, Micky?"

Micky looked at her and then looked at Brad. He pulled the gun out and pointed it at Carla's face. He didn't speak for a minute and then pointed it at Brad's face.

"Drink your beer, Carla," Micky said. "We are back together again, babe."

Carla was shaking. She finished the rest of her beer.

"Now, Brad," Micky said, "you're a very lucky man. I'm going to let you go. You don't know anything about what's gone on, and that's good. So, you see, when we have gone, you can do as you please. Maybe go back to Vegas, whatever you fucking want, but you've got no money and no Carla. You can go back to your fucking hotel work. I don't fucking care."

Micky looked at Carla and saw her slumped down in the chair. Micky's head started to spin. "Carla, are you okay?" he asked.

"No. I feel weak and dizzy," she mumbled as she fell to the floor.

Micky slumped down on the bed, feeling sick, weak, and dizzy. The gun dropped down by his side. Brad walked over to him and picked up the gun.

"You see … what it is *Micky* … I left you two on your own last night at the bar, so you could both plan your own downfall. I knew you would try and stitch me up. You are both greedy, and you deserve each other. I thought I would drug you both. Did you enjoy your beers? It won't kill you, but it will make you sleep for a few hours, so it's good night, Michael—or is it Micky? Who fucking cares?" He then leaned over and whispered in Micky's ear. "Never trust a man with an honest face, Micky. Now I will leave with the money, and you can have Carla."

CHAPTER 28

DRUGGED

Hours later, Micky had finally started to wake up. He quickly realized he'd been drugged, Carla too. He was groggy. He stumbled to his feet, shaking his head. He looked at his watch. It was nine o'clock in the evening. He'd been out for about nine hours. Micky looked around for Carla and found her lying on the floor, still out cold. He went over to her and knelt down beside her.

"Carla, wake up … Wake up, Carla." He slapped her face gently. "Carla, Carla … Wake up."

She finally started to groan and moved her head. Micky went to get her a glass of water. He cradled her in his arms. "Come on, Carla. Wake up, babe. Come on, babe."

She looked up at Micky and said, "I'm sorry, Micky. It's all my fault."

"Come on, Carla. Get to your feet. We've both been drugged. Let's see if we can get you walking."

Carla staggered around the room, holding on to Micky. "Keep walking, babe. Keep walking," Micky said.

"I'm ok now," she said. "I'm starting to feel better. My head's clearing. What about you, Micky? Are you all right?"

"I'm okay," Micky said. "If I find him, I'll fucking kill him."

"Me too," Carla said. "I'll kill him with you. We'll kill the fucker together. I'll stomp on his balls—just like the old days, Micky."

"Everything's gone," Micky said, searching the room. "The money, everything."

The couple headed out on to the hotel balcony and looked down to see if the cars were still there.

"It's gone … He's took the money and Carla's car. Shit!" shouted Micky.

Micky looked at Carla. "Is that the rental car he's taken?"

"Yes, it is," replied Carla. "And he's taken all the money as well."

Micky looked at her and paused to thinks for a minute. "I've got an idea. I have a friend who might be able to trace it."

"But how?" Carla asked.

"How do you think I found you, Carla?" replied Micky. "Have you got Brad's mobile phone number?"

Carla got her phone out and looked up Brad's number. She passed it to Micky, and he then called the number.

"No one is answering," he said. He looked out over the balcony and screamed. "I'm coming to get my revenge on you, Brad. Believe me, I'm coming to fucking get you, Brad. I'll fucking kill you! I'll shoot your balls off!" Micky was screaming in a rage. "You piece of fucking shit!"

He looked at the phone and started texting.

"What are you texting, Micky?" Carla asked.

He sent the message to Brad's phone and then showed the phone to Carla. The text read: "Murder by pencil."

Printed in Poland
by Amazon Fulfillment
Poland Sp. z o.o., Wrocław